CU00895054

All The Little Places

All The Little Places

SOPHIE SHILLITO

BLUE MARK BOOKS

First published in Great Britain by
Blue Mark Books Limited in 2020

www.bluemarkbooks.com

A catalogue record for this book is
available from the British Library

ISBN 978-1-910369-20-3

Blue Mark Books Limited supports the Forest Stewardship Council®. The
FSC® promotes the responsible management of the world's forests.
All our books carrying the FSC® logo are printed on FSC®-certified paper

Typeset in Adobe Caslon Pro by
Blue Mark Books Limited

Printed and bound by
CPI Group (UK) Ltd, CR0 4YY

For Freddie, who loves trains.

The Beginning

This is the beginning. This is how it starts.

Here are the people and the fragments of their lives. Here are their songs and rhythms. Here is the man with teeth made from gold and the woman with the painted face. Here is the man who can't fall asleep, and the woman dressed for her funeral. Here they are, all of them. Their flesh, their secrets, their futures and their pasts.

They all wear black this morning, in enough shades to paint each room in the big house. The black her mother used to wear when she sold flowers for the dead, a golden cross hanging from her neck. The glossy black of the children's dog that found the body swinging in the wood. The rotten black canker growing inside the woman with the lump. Black like the ocean the whale cannot find.

Here is the train bound for the city, a shuttle in a loom. Here are all the photographs, taken from the window – slides in a carousel. Here is the church and the field. Here is the wood filled with darkness and the cemetery filled with the dead. Here are the flats, and the meat in the market. Here is the river to float it out to sea. Here are all the little places. This is how it goes.

The Station

Here is the station. People huddle in groups under the platform awning. The winter cold has weakened the sun and it rises meekly, shivering and shrunken.

Inside the ticket office, a woman screeches into the tannoy microphone. *Stand back behind the yellow line!* Rage boils in her throat. Her colleague on the platform wears a high-visibility vest fastened over his distended stomach. He pulls his lanyard from the crease of flesh under his chin. His breath smells of the morning and of the cigarette he sucked down in the car park, drawing heavily on it until he could feel the heat from the lit end on his fingers. He blew out a grey blanket knitted in his lungs, coughed up a wet lump and spat it on the frozen ground. A pigeon flew down, pecked and swallowed.

The tapeworm inside him is growing longer, eating the food he feeds it. It enjoys the cake and crisps and lemonade, and the milk he drinks in the middle of the night, straight from the bottle in the fridge which lights up the kitchen. It swallows all the meaty morsels sawn off his kebab, and the yellow peppers too. He can hear it thinking now, deep inside him, asking for more. His heart is blackened – the tubes blocked with the bacon dripping he pours from the pan to eat cold, spread on bread. The blackness has grown too big. His heart is too full and he will feel it stop as he grips the countertop with his fingers. The colour of his face will change from pink to purple as he prays to a long-neglected god before sliding onto the chipped lino. The last thing he will see is the dirt that needs sweeping from under the freezer.

The orange neon platform display is a beacon in the winter morning, telling stories about the places where the train will stop: greens, woods, orchards full of fruit trees, boughs sagging with purple plums – all eaten, all gone.

After the glittering cold cruelty of the platform comes the warm fug of the carriage. Labourers spread their legs wide and grunt back thick mucus stuck in their noses and throats. Their overalls are covered with the dirt of the previous day. Stale sweat gathers humidly above them as they rasp their chapped hands over unshaven whiskers.

One of them has a cough that won't go away. It escapes from him, spluttering round the carriage, landing on seat backs and rucksacks, and in the hair of the woman with the oversized tortoiseshell glasses. He slumps against the window. The empty stare on his gaunt face tells the story of his night – tumbled round in sweat-drenched sheets, threads twisted round a spindle. The green illuminated numbers on the clock said one and two and three and four, and he counted out the rhythm of the darkness on all his fingers and toes as his mouth grew drier and a car revved in the street outside. Finally, dawn reached through the curtain to grip his sickly face with her claws.

People breathe fetid air through their mouths. Every last droplet of condensation fogging the windows is saturated with malady. This is how disease spreads. A man afraid of inhaling his fellow passengers wears a dark cotton mask over his nose and mouth – a macabre surgeon, hiding his face from the world.

The woman sitting next to him has swathed her body in cheap fabric cut in the pattern of a dress. Underneath, she is a grotesque oil painting, a fleshy portrait – great slabs of meat on a mattress, red hams on a canvas. She rattles a bottle of pills down her throat and checks her wristwatch.

Whistles are blown, signals lowered.

The Village

It's a middling kind of place. The people live in creaky houses and visit the fishmonger on Fridays. There's a shop, and a butcher, a parish noticeboard carrying messages about cleaning services and small rodents for sale, and a playground where a plastic ride-on horse is spring-coiled into bark chippings. On Sundays, the clock on the church tower says eleven and the bell in the steeple chimes in agreement. The song of the bell bounces off the red-tiled houses and echoes in the wood, waking the nocturnal animals.

When the weather is warmer, the men hoist a colossal tent on the village green, heave-ho-ing and striking at oversized pegs with wooden mallets, sweating, swearing and finishing in the pub, the one with the picture of a bull swinging outside.

The following day, the morning sun throws long shadows on the dew-soaked grass. The people slather sun cream on the backs of their creased leather necks, under wide-brimmed straw hats. Women march in dirndl skirts as floral and wide as couch cushions, scuffing their sensible shoes across the lawn, carrying ruby red pots of jam. Queen sponges are held high – whisked, whipped, baked and buttercreamed. Tombola tickets revolve in the drum, and a breeze slaps spotted cloth bunting against the plastic doors of the tent, in time with the accordion. Children grow fractious on sugary sweets lucky-dipped from the sawdust barrel and run off to poke sticks into the dead crow lying in the lane.

When the village was younger, its heart beat louder, in time with the pound of the farrier's irons. The railway came like an arrow from the city, cleaving hillsides in two. Trees were chopped down with shining axes. The station was built with bricks and iron, and the people hung the name of their village proudly on the wall.

Now, the railway chiefs keep ordering the underpass to be repainted, and another layer of industrial white is daubed on the tunnel walls where it seeps into the bricks. They drip with damp and inevitably, predictably, peel and flake again. It smells down there, always. Men ride the late train home, up to their elbows in paper bags of greasy chips, shovelling them, with fat fingers, into the redness of their mouths, inhaling them in a gulp as big as a whale, burping loudly as they alight. Suit flies are unbuttoned, and pale, limp slugs shrivel in the night air as the men leak into the underpass corners, sighing with a relief they can see – steaming white lung clouds, reflected in the convex corner mirror at the foot of the stairs.

Huge hams dried with salt from a foreign sea hang high above the butcher's head. His whites are pasted with brown animal liquids, wiped absent-mindedly on his bib. A mongrel lies in a stained basket behind the counter – born years ago on a soft pink towel in the cupboard under the stairs, his tiny heart an eyelid flutter. Blindly, he had pawed his mother's teat, sucked out the yellow milk and whimpered. Old now, his hairy snout is rough silver. He knows the smell of each loyal customer: soot from a fire, buttery toast, the salty river.

The butcher knows how to hold the animals and how to gut them, how to cut away the fat and sinew, where their fleshy bellies hide. His father taught him, in the same shop, behind the red and white chainmail curtains, before the arthritis deformed his hands so he couldn't hold a cleaver and he had to sit in the back, in the bath chair, wondering what his children would do with his own flesh when he died.

When the wheezy old man finally stopped breathing, his scabby grandchildren flytipped the chair into the ditch by the side of the track. It's still there, lying next to an old case clock. Every day at twenty past five, the hexagonal face is correct – at teatime when the children come home from school, and in the morning when the first light creeps across the horizon, and fox cubs visit. They sniff at the numbers, telling the time that men made – a time different to the up and down of the sun and the turning of the earth to make the seasons.

Beyond the ditch is a terrace of smart brick palaces built for captains of industry. The gardens are laid out in rectangles. Here are the spaces where prize flowers are grown for the horticultural competition, and a plastic slide and swing set is installed overnight as a birthday surprise. Where trays of cool lemonade and cheese straws are brought from laminate kitchens. Where the bushes are carefully clipped with secateurs, and a washing line spins in a circle between a miniature pond and a chemically treated fence. Workaday shirts for the week hang out to dry – bodies swinging in the breeze of the winter morning – stiff and starchy. One to wash, one to wear, one to put in the drawer.

The woman who lived in the cul-de-sac by the church hadn't been well for a while. Ever since her baby was born. One day last year when her husband was at work, she walked out of her house, leaving the door open and the baby at home. She entered the shop, making the bell ring. The sound echoed round the shelves displaying packets of stale pink iced biscuits and cans of soup older than their sell-by dates, rousing the man who lives in the room at the back. He rolled off his tired mattress and came out of his hiding place – an ogre emerging from his cave at the end of winter.

When the woman returned home her baby was gone, stolen by a stranger. He was so beautiful – a mop of fine black hair on top of his head, like he had been dangled upside down in an inkwell. She had loved the idea of him so much. Right from the very beginning, when first there wasn't and then there was. Time had changed from empty to full – magic and science and love came together in a triangle to make life. She couldn't stop looking at the photograph taken at the hospital. Her future, printed in black and white. Pixels on paper telling a truth she couldn't yet see with her eyes or touch with her hands, but could feel in her belly and knew in her heart. A tiny baby, made in the quiet space after midnight.

After he was taken she stood on the track in the small light of dawn, waiting for the first train to plough her down. She listened for it coming and felt it in her legs and feet just before it rounded the bend – the waggon of death, coming to finish her. She looked the driver in the eye and grinned at him with sweet relief.

These days, a single candle burns in the window of her house, where her husband keeps a vigil. He looks at the candle and thinks of the animals who gathered round the baby born in their byre, and of the old men who brought trinkets and perfume that the baby paid no mind to. When the animals grew too slow and gristly, a shepherd carved fatty lumps from their bodies with a golden sword, melted them in a pot on a fire made from the forest, and poured the liquid into a mould, making a candle just like the one in the window, burning for the world and all the people in it.

The Church

Here is the church, here is the steeple, a fat golden dragon spies all the people.

Above the church clock lies a dragon, beaten out of earth metal and snipped into shape. A talisman, made to ward off others of her kind who would breathe fiery flames in through the doorways of the thatched houses, burning the babies in their wicker cribs and taking livestock from the barn like meat from a larder – creeping through the village, plucking the vicar from the vestry and wives from their hiding places, swallowing each one down long scaled throats.

This dragon sails on a gilded compass. The wind decides which way she will look. Blown to the east, the dragon sees the sea, and the sea sees her. Blown to the west, the dragon sees the countryside laid out before her, shaken and landed – antique linen on a table. Here are the people, walking to the station. The long metal track leads past the field and the big house, then the wood, over the hill and far away. The dragon sees the city in the distance, filled with the blood of men.

In the porch of the church is a map of the village and the land around it. It is old, framed by a golden rectangle. The edges of the map mark the edges of knowledge. Beyond the edges, darkness: faraway places, unknown territories, imagined and feared. Look – there is the church in the middle of the map, a dark, crossed orb. There is the big house, drawn in red and spelled out in black letters, black as the walls are now. The estate is larger and the map maker has drawn a kitchen garden in the space where the pool should be. Miniature ink turnips and gourds grow in the earth. The train has not come yet; it is not time. The field is a square and the wood is a shape painted green, meeting the boundary of the estate. In the middle of the wood are the animals, circling the pond.

Below the map a long brass plate is set into the floor, put there in a time before anyone can remember. A body is buried beneath, hidden below the gleaming metal, which shows a picture of a knight wearing armour and chain-mail, his sword clasped tightly with two gloved hands. The village children slip through the porch doorway, pressing paper and rubbing the knight with wax sticks, making versions of him in red and purple.

Twin sisters wake at the same moment in the night, breathing quietly in their shared bedroom, lying in twin beds with twin blankets over their legs. Each sister can feel the other is awake but neither speaks; they are both too afraid. The older one – born four minutes first – reaches out across the narrow gap between the beds to hold hands. The purple knight stands above their headrests, stuck with tape to the wall, watching over them, keeping them safe. He will use his sword if he has to.

Tiny golden stars pierce the ceiling of the church, printed onto the blue plaster by a painter who lay on his back at the top of a towering scaffold. He had a taste for crab apples and an eye for the verger's daughter, despite their difference in age.

A man comes in and takes off his shoes and socks. He places his bare feet on the chiselled flagstone tomb of a stranger and gasps as his toes touch the icy slab. His breath vibrates round the walls. *Can you feel me*, he says out loud, *standing on top of you?* He bends his body at the knees and prays with his eyes closed against the world, his hand resting on the back of a pew, feeling the wood worked by the carpenter who turned the trees to make seats for God. Birds perch in the rafters and shower droppings on the floor, covering the words carved into it. The man is startled by the noise and opens his eyes. His tongue stops praying and he lifts his head to the ceiling to see the stars that remind him of the ones he looks at through his telescope.

When the sun sets over the village, he takes his instrument from the hallway and walks out into the field. He looks through the viewfinder up into the dark blue sky, searching for celestial bodies high in the firmament. He sees the princess, turned upside down in her electric chair, watching the last trains bringing the people home.

On Sundays, the vicar welcomes her flock, who stand when she tells them to stand, and sit when they are bidden, singing the hymns vigorously and worshipping a god they cannot see.

A pink-faced couple hold hands discreetly in a pew at the end of the nave. He grips her fingers tightly with his. He has her, his prize, captured. She promised with a ring, in this church, to be his. Forever. Last night they lay side by side on their mattress, and she thought of the carved marble monarchs lying down by the altar – a king and his queen adorned with matching crowns. The queen made a promise with a ring in the church, and the king gripped her fingers tightly with his.

Out in the churchyard, a woman sits on a bench, pressing her hands together round a coffee flask – a caffeinated prayer. She wears her mother's fat golden crucifix on a leather cord. The shining metal shape presses her skin, branding her a child of God. The cord is a black necklace of belief, choking her doubt back down with her bile, worry and regret; strangling her guilt like a soft snowy animal. She reads a book written by God in the time when God was a man and walked the earth with the livestock and the women who tended them. It is a book of songs and letters. The text is small and the verses are long, and the woman squints to understand them. Here is the story about the dancer who cut off the preacher's head and served it up for dinner. Here is the story about the feathered man, sent from heaven as a warning.

The Field

In the space between the village and the wood, right before the big house, lies the field. Village, field, big house, wood – that's how it goes – blurred brown sticks and stones, grass, glimpses, shutter frames.

In the warmer months, the clever cuckoo watched the little brown bird on her nest and waited, waited, in the shadow of the field grass, until she flew away, showing the cuckoo the clutch of four blue-speckled beauties. The cuckoo saw her chance and flew to the nest, pushing her own egg through her cloaca into the down-filled twig circle. *Just the same*, thought the cuckoo, *an identical twin*, and she laughed to herself as she flew away, knowing her hatched baby would be king when he crawled from the yolky hole.

That morning, three huge balloons rose high above the field – red, blue and orange. Children from the village – up early with the cattle – came to watch. Flames as fierce as the lion painted into the plaster wall of the church roared from the burners, bloating the slumped sacks with heated air. The men climbed into the baskets and cut away the ropes, untethering their ships. They sailed upwards, stately, and the children waved and ran underneath as the men soared over the big house, over the wood, and across the countryside, using the track to show them the way.

At the end of the summer, the machines came – first one, then another, cutting the field crop with whirring blades and champing metal mouths that tore the yellowed plants from the earth and spat them into the hopper. Field mice and voles ran terrified into the wood, leaving their babies screaming from straw nests which were shredded and scattered in one bite. The clatter and thrum moved to the edges of the field, leaving a churned wake. Birds flew above, black winged and hopeful, scanning the soil for the day's catch.

The stutter of a startled cock pheasant split the air. Magnificently stupid, overstuffed on the feed from the barrels which he had gobbled down his regal gullet. Before dawn, the men set off from the village, black dogs following them, whining in the darkness. The morning was heavy with the scent of wet animals and wax jacket. The men wore bird tails in their hats and fired at their quarry, and the dogs held the warm feathered bodies gently in their mouths, down caught between their teeth. The men took the birds by their throats, grasping them between hardened fingers – four in each hand, swinging back and forth.

Now, the cut ends of the field crop stubble over the earth's surface, pushing up through the frost-hardened ground. Across the carriage, a man pulls a dinted metal tin from the soft darkness of his coat pocket. Inside is the brightest yellow tobacco. He sniffs it and pokes a little into the pouch of his cheek.

The winter moon won't go to bed. It's a day moon, a night-time ghost haunting waking hours, looming over the field. Mist hangs low, a jellyfish undulating above the ground, translucent and floating. It moves around the legs of the cattle, giving them a tulle petticoat to wear, hiding their ankles. They stand together round a trough, hooking mouthfuls of straw with their pink tongues.

In the middle of the field is the lightning tree – a dead oak, an amputee pugilist fighting the air. The silent shriek of the trunk is shocking and sounds like war – sodden grey trenches, countryside turned to mire. The storm came in the darkest chapter of the night, pouring its fury on the people, who rose from their beds and tiptoed in bare feet across to windows, pushing back curtains and opening shutters to watch the lightning and hear the thunder, one then the other, one then the other. A woman was jolted from sleep. Lightning. Each flash brighter than the last. She lay stiffly still, anticipating the thunder, fearful. It arrived, loud and menacing – an army approaching from a distance, a tidal wave, a monster in the dark, using the lightning to find her. Another flash. She counted under her breath: *one, two, three, four, five, six* – thunder again. Six miles away. Lightning. Again she counted: *one, two, three, four* – thunder, coming closer, unstoppable, seeking her out in her bed. She pulled the blankets tight around herself, listening. Rain knocked on her window – a drumbeat to welcome the thunder, to tell it where she lay.

Rolling over the wood, the storm woke the animals, who stirred deep in their burrows and shuffled through dry grasses to the mouths of their chambers, smelling the electric air and hearing the rain fall on the earth outside their setts and holes. Reaching the field, the storm did its worst, pointing one electric finger straight at the earth and cursing, striking the oak and setting it alight – an evil spell flung from the end of a wand.

At dawn, a man walked out to look at the smouldering stump and swept the wet earth with his detector, swinging it from left to right in front of his rubbered feet, listening to the sounds it made – the sounds of the soil, the sounds of the past, beeping through the loam and the centuries. He pinpointed the noise like a bat using sonar, crouched quickly, and dug. There, at the bottom, was the coin, small and blackened with age. The man took it in his fingers and rubbed to see the ancient portrait, put it in his corduroy pocket and smiled at his secret.

The Big House

Long ago, the family who lived in the big house planted a thorn hedge around the edges of the estate, marking the boundary between what was theirs and the common land. Seven miles long and fifteen feet high – a prickly barrier so tall no man would dare leap over it, even with a barrel of beer in his belly. The raggedy remains border the track, prickling over the hill to the wood.

Animals lived in the hedge and thrived. Small birds perched on the branches, singing sweet songs they heard when they flew in through holes in the church roof, and others they borrowed from the maids who gathered herbs to strew on wooden floors.

There's an old man living in the village who remembers the last party. Light from the open doorway spilled over the step and down the gravel driveway, rutted by the wheels of carts and cars. The light was yellow and inviting and carried the sound of glasses clinking like tiny bells, and laughter from the pearl-coated throat of a woman who was older than she looked. She smelled of cloying perfume pumped from a glass bottle cut in the shape of a heart.

A dog barked rudely at guests announced by the butler at the beginning of the evening and dismissed with a wave of his white-gloved hand at the end. There was music from a violin, played by a boy fetched from the jungle, his instrument carved by his father to fit under his chin.

Men brought ice from the ice house, rolling up their shirt-sleeves and stepping inside the moist brickwork dome, feeling the change in temperature on the bare skin of their arms as they crossed the threshold, like the cold in a tunnel cut through a mountain. They shovelled the ice into a barrow and wheeled it through the formal beds and borders, around the parterre and past the pool to the kitchen steps. It glittered in the moonlight – a precious cargo set sail across the garden, hard as the diamonds on the gnarled right hand of a duchess, who scooped sorbet with a golden spoon between the courses of sole and ox cheek.

In the years immediately before the fire, fewer and fewer members of the family lived in the house – moving away to the city, taking ships to hotter places where they cut their way through jungles in search of seeds that would make their fortunes. Those that remained became frightened to enter the library, haunted by the housekeeper's story about an uncle who reached too far, high on the wheeled staircase. It slipped out from under him, leaving him gripping a tall bookshelf which had never been properly screwed into the wall, and fell on top of the man, crushing him underneath, his huge brain staved in with a volume of his own work.

The wheels shriek a melancholy whistle as the train rounds the bend – metal on metal. The ghost of the house stands on the brow of the hill, silhouetted against the winter sunrise, light shining through the empty rooms, fiercely, like the fire that night. The smoke could be seen from miles away – grey-orange, rising in the east. The house smells of soot and ashes now – charred wood remains where, once, blonde-haired children ran their fingers over carved oak panelling cut from the trees in the wood and chiselled by the carpenter, who had a simple name. The housemaid liked to rub beeswax into the panels with a soft cloth, filling the air with the smell of honey from the hives in the kitchen garden – borage and sweet cicely.

The boy who lived in the house awoke to see the fire reaching its pointed fingers under his bedroom door. He felt a heat hotter than the volcano in his schoolbook that turned the people to stone. Smoke blackened the air and fear soaked the sheets as the boy held his breath and lay down in the shape of a stone boy, crossed his fingers and waited for the lava.

A child stands on the lawn, watching the train go by at the bottom of the estate. He is barefoot, wearing only his bedclothes. A woman on the train raises her hand and presses it to the window. The boy holds his aloft in return and for a shared moment they are locked together in a time which is not the past and not the present.

The summer after the fire, the looters came – in the night, and then more boldly in the day – taking melted golden objects: a linnet cage, fused knives from the cutlery drawer, a lump made from hat pins, the twisted tuning fork, scorched portraits of the sepia family. Animals padded softly through the rooms, across the blackened parquet floor of the study and up the stairs to the wide landing, where the heir – unable to escape through the flames – had taken his father's pistol and pressed it hard and quickly to the roof of his mouth, spattering himself against the velvet curtains.

Teenagers from the village – mouths wet with beer and kisses – crept up to the house through the estate, running through the dense foliage of plants brought from other lands on great ships, their huge white sails pointing the way home. They undressed without ceremony and jumped in pencil dives straight down through the water, swimming up to break the surface, laughing and gasping.

The water turned green. An algae skin grew on the pool surface and on the ceramic tiles, ruining the painted motif which had echoed the oceanic frieze above the picture rail in the octagonal hallway. Shells fetched from warm seas – clams and mussels, razors and sea snails – swam in synchronicity round the gallery, dancing a routine to music they all knew, a flute and drum counting them round.

The pool is dry now and filled with rotting leaves. The bolts holding the metal ladder in place have come loose and the steps hang off their fixings at a drunken angle. A dozen great beauties stood on those steps, up to their knees in the water, toenails perfectly painted. They plunged elegantly into the turquoise bath, swimming caps bobbing above matching woollen swimsuits. They played croquet all summer long, hitting ball after coloured ball through hoops on the lawn as a way to pass the time during the afternoons, before the heat of the day lost its ardour and the sun slunk down behind the wood, chasing stars from their daytime hiding places and trading turns with the moon. Night-times were filled with cocktails, and cars piled high with women in fringed dresses sitting giddily on the laps of men who stiffened and sprang beneath them as they drove into the city, seeking dark pleasures.

The Wood

Here is the wood. Here is the place the man was found hanging, swinging slowly in the breeze. He had scouted for the best place – an easy climb and a sturdy branch with a long drop. The village children found him, blue and bloated. They dared each other to pull the socks from his feet and put them on their hands to make woollen mouths that said *run away*. A bird beguiled them with its song: crotchets and a minim written on the air, a sweet trill they could see, black flies buzzing around a corpse, drowsy and engorged.

Water fills a hole dug out by men – not with machines, or tools, but with their strong, blistered hands, long ago, when the trees were saplings and light shone through the sparse canopy onto the earthen floor. People call it the cowpond, too innocent to know the truth about how or why it was dug. The men waited for days until the sky broke, sending rain down on the wood. Fat droplets fell on the leaves, making a thousand prisms, and the hole became an evil font. Not for baptism, no. For drowning. The men saw the pond and smiled to themselves, their trap complete.

Years later, when the north wind blew the animals deep into their dens, the drowning pond froze over. Frogs and fish were trapped in an icy grave – shaped novelties in a chilled soup. Men came from the big house with axes and picks that glistened in the winter air, and brought them down on the lid of the pond to smash the ice with a crack that resounded through the trees. Back at the house, the maid placed tall iced drinks on a golden tray and pulled the dumb waiter's ropes to make it slide up to the ground floor, where the handsome butler would unload it like he was opening a birthday present.

Horses run in the wood. Luminous, glowing white against the darkened spaces, moving between the trees, faster than the train. Something has frightened them – their eyes are wild, and they sweat hard through their flanks as they gallop away. At the beginning of winter, one of them was found in the pond's thick flotsam. Bloated and grey, filled with a pungent gas that puffed it up like a frightened fish and held it at the top of the water, revolving slowly under the yellowed sky. The woman who lives in the wood found its shivering foal and very gently placed her knobbly thumb in the dappled velvet groove between its eyes.

The people catch sight of her from a distance sometimes, when they walk their dogs. If they go near, she hisses at them through broken teeth. Her tumbledown shack lets the rain in. Inside, there's a low-slung bed, and an old wooden wine box on the floor with a tin tray on top, holding her household relics: a horse's tooth, a tiny plastic train fallen out of a cracker, a musty prayer book, a thimble inlaid with red rubies, a small framed photograph of a sailing ship, and a lock of hair.

At night-time, in the hours after the electric lights in the house at the end of the village are turned off, before the first pale blue sliver of tomorrow shows itself above the frozen field, the great carnival begins. The foxes rise first, stepping in time. The furry paws of the weasels leave tiny imprints on the earth as they parade round the drowning pond, mesmerised by the reflection of mother moon. A white hare drums a rhythm with its hind foot in time with the heartbeats of the trees, waking the mice in their straw nests at the field edge, calling them to join the dance. Owls fly on silent wings, singing the song of the night.

The Chalk Pit

The view changes as the landscape becomes wider – watercolour sky floods the window, framing the unwanted things collecting in the chalk pit. Old record players dumped on the sodden cushions of a three-seater sofa, brown fabric worn and unravelling. Hundreds of rusting things, and a gallery of glazed prints, faded by the sun.

A tree grows through the floor of a burnt-out car. Boys poured petrol from a can onto the patterned seats. They soaked rags, holding them aloft like beacons, and threw them through the passenger window, watching the fire engulf the steering column and melt the plastic sun visors.

Thousands of years ago, hunters discovered the cave at the back of the pit and lay down on the dusty floor, listening to the darkness and the wind moving past the open hole, singing a melody. Creatures came, first alone then in pairs, sniffing the scent of them on the wind. Torch flames licked the walls, illuminating painted stories. Wild cats stalked the land, pouncing on weasels and devouring them, dragging bigger prey into the cave. The sound of teeth on bone echoed round the craggy walls, bouncing off stalactite fingers clinging to the ceiling.

There are clouds above the chalk pit today – a majestic mountain range. The sun highlights the rugged cracks and spurs. A man on the train opens the hole in his old face to smile at them, as he thinks of the mountain he was born on. He shows all his teeth, worn and golden – tiny lumps of sugar.

His grandmother was an ice woman – she lived in the land of darkness and fire, where the days are shortest. The sun went to bed after lunch and didn't get up until long past the time the dogs were barking in the yard. On her mantelpiece was a felted swan, stitched together with a needle and thread by candlelight, in her kitchen, in the wooden mountain house. Wolves howled outside and the townspeople prayed to an old god. The swan winked its black button eye. That night the glacier skulked down the mountain, dragging a wake of rocks and gravel, licking the scree slope with its icy tongue, crystallising the tiny winter flowers and freezing the ground under its belly. Blue with cold, it poured itself on the town, slithering over the people in their beds, rolling and trapping their stiff bodies in an icy cocoon.

Until he was old enough to grow a beard, the man lived

at the top of the mountain, in the high meadows under the ridge, near the border where one country becomes another. He washed himself in a cold stream and ate blueberries picked from the bushes. He squeezed hot, sweet milk from the teats of animals into a metal cup, drank it quickly and wiped away the white moustache with the sleeve of his machine-knitted jumper. He watched vultures with feathered hoods hollowing out a dead cow lying by the side of the lake – pulling out liver, spleen and lungs to make a red grotto as the blood dried in a sticky pool on the grass.

One afternoon, when the spring sun shone on the lake, the man climbed down to it and dropped his clothes at the water's edge. He stood on a rock in the shallows, listening to a hawk screaming down the valley. He swam out to a small island – the water was shallow and his toes tangled in the soft green weed. A dragonfly darted low – turquoise and prehistoric.

The Common

Lately, big cracks have appeared on the common, zigzagging their way across the land, revealing the earth beneath – layers of soil and clay, small pieces of rock and hundreds of beetles, surprised by the daylight. Hard-hatted men from the council have been to look – peering down into the fissure, making notes on their clipboards, taking measurements with a long retractable tape.

Sometimes a carnival stops here. At night, the carnival people light a bonfire, huge and red. Lusty devils rise from the underworld, tonguing the bottom of the sky, sniffing for blood and the bare breasts of women. Black paper marionettes fastened with golden split pins dance round wax-crayoned flames. Great plumes of smoke fill the freezing air, tickling the lungs of the people, who fall asleep on goose down pillows with the smell of fire in their hair.

In their dreams, the ringmaster laughs, showing the place he hides handkerchiefs, and cracks his whip hard on the dirt floor of the ring. The sound makes the monkeys move in a circle, each combing fleas from the back of the next. In the cabin beside the big top, an apron-clad woman makes proper cups of tea, dunking round teabags into water that's the perfect temperature – hotter than a bath and cooler than a boiling tar pit. Then the milk, just enough to turn the tea a good colour. It needs to be tanned and strong, like the arms of her first husband, who died at sea. She plucks a sausage from the grill with her long purple claws, plops it into a bun and squeezes yellow mustard over its flaccid body. The strong man inhales it in one suck – sauce gathers at the sides of his rubbery mouth, which asks for *another, darling, please.*

The train passes yellow freight waggons filled with coal – hard black diamonds dug from deep in the earth, ancient treasure.

A woman with wet-look curls pokes furiously at her face. Her fingers are loaded with a fine mineral powder scraped from a rich palette of feminine colours: pig pink, vulva pink, kiss pink, glorious foetal pink – to cover the lesions, to hide her hideousness from the world. She uncaps a greasy stick and pastes the red on her lips, layer on layer, until she is rouged, gaudy and proud, and draws back her lips to smile the smile of a clown – bloody oil across her teeth.

She dabs away sweat which smells of the cheap alcohol she drank too quickly last night. In the pub toilet, she had looked at herself in the mirror for too long. The face staring back was no longer hers. All the sinews in her neck writhed like the limbs of the dead in a plague pit. She could see her skull under the flesh, eye sockets wide, and the roots of her teeth showed through the side of her jaw. Just as fast, the bones disappeared, and she returned to the bar.

Afterwards, she ran for the train home, struggling in

her too-tall shoes through the wintered streets, losing one on the steps. On the train she fetched another drink from her oversized bag, clicking the ring-pull with a lacquered acrylic nail. Before she could drink it, she fell asleep, filled up to the brim with cans of sugared liquor in a range of pastel colours the marketing bosses said would appeal to her demographic. They were right. She drank them down, swallowing the pale lemon yellows – medicines that cured her ugliness and doubt for an evening, silenced the voices in her head and made her beautiful. Rosy vials lulled her into a sleep where not even dreams could trouble her as she sailed on past her stop, into the night, all the way to the sea.

The Cemetery

The train crosses the viaduct. Sprawling beneath is the cemetery, a last landscape, a garden of death, filled with corpses and decorated with the words of the living. Here, the people are lowered, stiff by stiff, into holes in the earth, hidden in the ground like secrets. Once, this place was a forest, where lions and wolves ate each other in turn, an eye for an eye.

Wives are widows and men are ghosts, planted rank and file – a mute soil regiment, smiling in the darkness. Roses feed on the last meals of the dead, blooming on the graves, even in the icy winter. Here is the doctor who could cure all ills, save for his own, which he could not diagnose. Here is the man who was found in the wood. Here is the boy who wasn't strapped in. Here is his twin. Here is the carpenter's wife, and her infant sons who died together inside her, whispering their final words in the red velvet darkness of her womb, dragging her with them under the earth.

Stone angels perch on the gravestones like birds come looking for breadcrumbs, feathered and flighty. From their roosts on the dead, they can see for miles – back and forth across the landscape, through generations and

lives. Stories and fragments are written on stone tablets –
sagas, lies and untruths, facts made myth, promises and
apologies carved into markers decorated with milk-bellied
cherubs.

The bushes are overgrown and under-tended, vast and sprawling. Here, men wrap themselves in whisky and grime-soaked bundles – lying low in the daytime and emerging with the crepuscular creatures at twilight. Crawling from their sleeping bags and breathing on the earth. Bad breath, which smells of sleep and scraps scraped from bins. An old pink sheet winds round twiggy branches and tangles in dead leaves, bearing the greasy grey imprint of a man who spent six days and six nights here, thinking he was dead. On the seventh day, his fever broke. He unwrapped his shroud, stepped out of the undergrowth, and vanished into the world.

A buzz cut teenage boy wears a slogan tee shirt – a word that means go away, get out, no thank you and not today. A word filled with meanness and meaning. A word he spits into the scrubby patches of bracken growing between the graves. He and his friends mark their territory like dogs, on the brick wall that borders their kingdom. They smoke fat joints of carefully rolled leaves, setting the ends alight and pulling the sweet, dark smoke down into their lungs, holding their breath and passing the parcel, until the music stops.

In the space between evening and morning, the boys slip silently along the track, betrayed only by shaken ball bearings inside their metal cans. They move unseen, stepping over rails and sleepers, seeking fresh surfaces, working secretly in the darkness. Shake and spray, silver paint shines in the moonlight – each boy writes his name over and over, until the meaning is lost and it is just a printed shape.

The woman leaning against the luggage rack lay next to her husband last night, watching him fall asleep before her. His eyes were closed and the blanket her mother had stitched was tucked under his chin, catching his breath as it formed small beads of moisture which balanced on the tiny woollen hairs like raindrops on blades of grass – whole worlds in jewelled spheres. His head looked like a death mask – plaster poured over a face, like the one she had seen in the city museum, trapped in a glass case.

Across the carriage, a man looks up from the poetry he's reading – laudanum rivers and beds soaked with disease, lovers clasping strings of pearls. He wears a rakish uniform – long coat, big boots, knotted chiffon scarf snagging on his Adam's apple. A cheap metal earring dangles coquettishly from the hole in his lobe, making him itch.

The Power Station

.

Alongside the track, pylons march across the land, swinging skipping ropes and singing, voices crackling with electric fire.

The train passes the huge gas-filled barrels. Vast tubes painted with stripes bend this way and that – serpents winding through a metal forest. Flames shoot from their heads as they move toxic, boiling liquids from one tank to another.

Bats hang upside down under the corrugated metal eaves of the roof, gripping tightly with their shiny claws and looking at the view. Later, when the land grows dark and all the lights in the city towers are turned on, they'll drop from their perches and soar in black leather clouds around the pipes, negotiating the smoke stacks, eating tiny insects on the wing.

The power station sizzles and steams, sewing people together on a patchwork grid that lights up the night.

In the flats, twin brothers living together in middle age take it in turns to use the power fetched down fat cables to make dinner in their beige kitchen. Yesterday, half of the pair served his brother meat and potatoes and himself potatoes and meat. They ate in a room with the blinds drawn and the lights down low, chewing each piece of meat sixty times and washing it down with small cups of orange squash.

A woman knocked on the door, saying she was a neighbour and all her lights were out. She had no money to pay the bill the power chiefs sent to her doormat in the hallway where the carpet underlay shows through – it dropped through her box like a fish falling from a tree after a storm, making a wet and final sound. They let her in, despite their better judgement, fed her children gingersnaps and gave her gifts of a candle, a piece of silver and a blanket, before they let her out into the night and returned to the kitchen to write *biscuits* on the list.

The Flats

Once upon a time, wedged between the power station and the hospital, there was an old hotel. The weathered clout-nailed sign said *En suite rooms with television*. Inside, a couple lay on the bed. Checked in, she made use of the en suite facilities, slipping on a new nylon nightie bought in a department store sale. She lay on top of the silky bed cover, looking up at the stippled ceiling, and asked him if he wanted to. He swigged beer from the bottle resting on his vest-covered belly hump and continued to stare at the television sports.

Not long after, the place was torn down, and developers squeezed every last piece of silver from every last inch of land to build a squat block, low-rise and modern – so close to the track that passengers can easily gawk through the windows. Here are the flats – little rooms filled with little lives.

A girl with beautiful curls jumps from the top bunk. She is a flying squirrel, suspended in mid-air, frozen in the snapshot instant. Her wall is covered with insect stickers. The empty piñata from last week's birthday party sits on her dressing table, a used husk. Her mother had blindfolded her and placed a brightly coloured bat in her hand. She had fumbled towards the stripy alpaca-shaped beast, garrotted with string and hanged in a doorway. On the carpet below, ten greedy faces had leered up at the girl, waiting like baby birds for the piñata to burst and rain intestinal candy into their open mouths.

Her father sits on a leatherette sofa opposite a huge screen mounted above a fireplace – a modern mirror, reflecting the world. He's on the edge of the seat cushion, palms pressed together, watching the breakfast news and praying for the starving children.

Tonight, all the families in the flats will draw the curtains and gather round tables, passing salt and pepper – a hundred dinners served in a hundred domestic theatres. Sausage and mash, pies, grey chops from a pig, watery cabbage, overcooked carrots, and a sponge pudding steamed too long. A small hot ball of suet and currants, wrapped in a muslin cloth. Breathing and sweaty, shrouded in swaddling to hide its doughy pallor – a wet parcel to mark the washed-out end of a day.

A woman in high-heeled feather-toed slippers stands on a stool, the old-fashioned kind with fold-out steps. She's trying to untangle a cobweb of tiny lights, bundled away too hastily when last year's festivities ended – once the last bony bit of bird had been scraped dry and the easy peel fruits had shrivelled in the heat of the lounge. She'll hang the lights round the sliding doors that lead out onto her balcony where she's already installed a plastic stable – a battery-operated deer with flashing antlers is visiting a baby lying in an illuminated crib.

In her pokey kitchen, she's hung the word *love* on the wall above the fridge. She wishes for love to come flying in through the window like a fat golden lark. The *o* in the *love* is heart-shaped and studded with more lights, which flicker on and off. The woman frowns and thinks about the faulty wiring, afraid it might set her flat alight – her home consumed by love. She climbs down from the stool, switches off the *love* and opens the fridge to eat the ham inside.

Near the top of the block is a sky jungle, a garden tower with a princess trapped inside, lying on the carpet. Her golden hair is plaited and woven with delicate green tendrils. She's planted bulbs in pots of earth – brown and silver tubers which shiver papery skin. She patted down the loam, burying them in living graves, and afterwards scrubbed soil from her nails with her lacquered wooden bristle brush painted with a picture of a small blue ship.

The bulbs are exploring their new home, a moist dark resting place to grow and clone, to sprout new babies that cling to their sides, wound tight in a papoose. Hairy roots crackle their way through the earth, feeling blindly for things to hold on to.

Below the princess, a man sits in the cool, quiet darkness of his dining room, looking into his aquarium. He wonders if his fish are related to the fish in the tank at his doctor's office – aquatic brothers and sisters, separated by the scoop of the pet shop net. Every night he writes about her in his diary, and prays for her, kneeling on the rug made from scraps of his old shirts and underpants.

Once, he found one of her long blonde hairs on his jacket. The idea of her soothes him. She listens and asks questions and writes things down with a small pencil she keeps in a jar that once held gooseberry jam. The fish swim up and down in the illuminated water, looking at him and listening to his stories, glad they are fish. The man looks at the fish and wishes he was a fish, a simple fish.

The Hospital

The train stops, held at a signal. One of the carriage windows frames the view outside. Disused warehouses, and a siding where concrete blocks and cables have been dumped amongst the weeds – couch grass and groundsel, moving in the wind. Here is the hospital, a lead-roofed brick edifice, older than the railway.

At the front of the carriage, the mousy woman touches herself under her coat. It's just a little lump – nothing to worry about, nothing to see. Just a little lump, buried deep in the fatty tissue, hidden and cankerous. At night she lies awake in the darkness of her room, feeling the lump and watching the beams from car headlights shine through her cheap curtains and travel across the ceiling. The lump grows bigger in the night-time. In the small hours of the morning, it swells large in her imagination, as she thinks about the people who will miss her when she's dead.

A man strap-hangs by the wheezy sliding doors, trying to forget the memory of last night's party. *Come on*, his hostess said, encouragingly, *come on, it will be fun – we'll all make newspaper hats.* Gaudy, sartorial cloches, ruched fascinators, broad-brimmed pirate tricornes. Each happy hat told a story – war, corruption, kidnap. His showed pictures of writhing patients, filled with trial injections for a new drug. Rashes had freckled across their fevered skin as they tore at their shirts, screaming about blindness. They were all paid for their time.

On the ward, a woman in a blue backless gown lies under the covers. Life has drawn creases on her beautiful face. A nurse has turned her bed towards the window so she can watch the trains go by, witnessing the world in which she once lived. She quivers benignly, her hand on the counterpane never quite still. Someone has painted her nails – bright red, like she used to do for herself until the trembling got bad, then worse, and she wet herself in the dairy isle of the supermarket. Her daughter said she would be better off being cared for by strangers – a captive trapped in a bed. Better there than sitting for days, alone, in a carpeted room, on the sofa with stretchy removable covers that could be washed at thirty degrees.

The moon will rise high above the hospital tonight. A silver nurse sailing over bedsides, taking temperatures and pouring drinks of moon juice, glittering in glasses left on nightstands. The patients are lulled by the moon. She is their mother, pressing a cool hand on fevered foreheads, rocking them on her crescent knee until they fall asleep.

The Market

After the hospital comes the market. A carrier bag falls open and shopping spills onto the floor of the train.

Under the domed plastic roof, people crowd around the stalls. Six chickens – run through with a cruel steel rod – rotate in a hot box. Pullets grown in a pitch-black stench, where dirt and guano had mixed with something darker, pecking gouges from their sisters' feathered breasts until pus oozed from the gaping wounds like garlic butter from a cutlet.

The vendor smells of meat. His large square mouth opens and closes like a mechanical wind-up toy, showing his gums, and his voice rises through the crowd as he calls out the prices of meat which get cheaper as the sun falls lower in the sky.

He plucked the birds, pulling out their stubby feathers like he was flaying angels. He chopped off their beaks and rubbery red combs, basted them with a brown sauce – a secret recipe made from herbs and dried fruit – and drove the metal spike through all their tiny hearts, cracking their breast bones as he made six wishes and roasted their skin.

His jumper creeps up above the waistband of his soft

trousers, revealing the place he was attached to his mother – a pale wet baby with palms spread, fingers pushing against the inside of her, feeling her spongy walls. He kicked against her, testing her resilience. She held the side of her body where her innards were bruised and purple, knowing she would need to push hard to deliver this one. He was stubborn and hooked his fingers into her opening, refusing to be born. The doctor had to prise him from her womb like a rabbit from a hole, by the scruff of his rolled, wrinkled neck.

The machine spits in disgust, dispensing purple notes at a man who bends over his bulging stomach to scoop them from the damp pavement. He waddles towards the flower stall to buy cheap carnations for his wife and roses for his girlfriend. He's a charmer all right – an old city wolf in heightening shoes, chewing on chalky indigestion tablets and smiling through his whitened teeth, stark against his winter tan. Saliva gathers at the corner of his mouth in creamy globs, and his stained, thinning hair, combed high on his head with a greasy pomander oil, is darker than the years have bleached him. A silky painted cravat caresses his turkey throat, loosely – he likes it that way, it reminds him of the sensual kiss of a lover, expensive and glamorous.

When he's not around, his girlfriend takes the hammer from her DIY set and balances it in her hand, feeling the weight of the metal. She wants to hammer her way out of her life, faster than the notes on a steel drum. This morning she wanted to drive the hammer through her skull. She's sick of pretending all night – bouncing on his flabby whiteness and calling him *papa*, testing her bed's wooden scaffold as she arches backward in ecstatic spasms

and throws herself against the bedroom wall in feigned delight at his thrusting and pumping, until he groans, shudders, and leaks into her.

The night will fall early. The earth is tilted away from the sun and the days are short, too short. The city will become shrouded in a darkness punctured with light – a black moth-eaten blanket. Holes reveal street lights and tail lights on taxis, lights shining from offices in towers and boats on the river.

The market alehouse will froth its patrons out onto the pavement – foam from a beer tap spilling into the street. Clouds of nicotine smoke will float upwards, mixing with the smell of pork frying on a skillet. Boys from the city wear a uniform: shiny suits that no longer fit their bodies, swollen fat on expense account lunches and bottles of whisky gifted by clients. Tonight they will grow rowdy-loud with liquor, high on the end of a week – spending fat envelopes of silver and swiping card after card through the machine until the woman at the bar calls *time please* and they ask for one more because they deserve it. They work so hard.

On Monday morning, they'll be back, gracing the new restaurant with their pretty pennies. Birds with hooked feet grip the pattern of leaves and fronds on the dark wallpaper. Beady yellow eyes stare at the bloated patrons as they slouch in leather wingback chairs. The cutlery is golden and the napkins crisp as snow. Eggs and kippers hide small pictures of pineapples painted on the plates. Waiters scuttle across the herringbone floor, bringing toasted bread with the crusts cut off, piled high in a teetering pyramid which the city boys slather with a thick layer of yellow butter.

Under the back stairs, in the basement of the building, there's a small cave of a kitchen. It's a hundred degrees down there, and the men – they are all men – take off their kitchen whites and work half-naked under buzzing strip lights, chopping, peeling, grilling, making creamy sauces. Boiling fat splashes their stomachs, bleaching skin and scarring the surface – pits in a landscape, barbed wire wounds on a tree. The youngest lives in a damp room and calls home once a week from the booth on the high road, coughing green bile from his spore-coated lungs.

Next door is the café, lagged in custard tiles and decorated with neon letters. The man inside has chosen a leather-ette bench facing the window and rests his elbows on the lemony table. The waitress arrives with his order, heels clicking on the tired lino. Scrambled eggs, and tea in a smoked glass mug. His hands close around it and he is comforted by the steamy heat. He bends his head forward and blows silently across the meniscus, lips pursed like he is playing a whistle, as he looks at the *Hot Bread* sign blinking on and off outside the bakery.

The baker sifts the flour – snow feathering into the big glass bowl. She mixes the dough and pummels it, hides it with a tea towel and leaves it on the windowsill to grow – creeping yeasty and unseen.

Queues form day and night for hot crinkle buns straight from the oven. Stuffed with shredded meat, mustard, and a slice of pickle – packed with a wink, brown-bagged and twirled, correct change and *next please*.

The River

The old, cold river seeps from under the city, thirstily seeking the light of the sun. The sea calls the water from the deep earth – *find me, join me.* The river bends through the sprawl, carrying the smell of locomotive diesel and unwashed people, fried meats and money.

The river is ancient. For a thousand years, eels, pike and waterworms, schooners and paddle steamers have floated in its waves.

Once, there were barges with crimson sails – red under-skirts fluttering in the breeze. Bargemen smacked the pewter water with wooden oars and churned it, causing more than a ripple as they rode the tide into the city, bringing wine and bricks, and hay for the horses.

Before them, a sea captain puffed out his hard, medal-covered chest and stood on deck – a flesh figure-head pointing the way. His ship sailed from the place where dates and tamarind grow, embarking in a different season to make a passage across waters filled with pirates and ice. The ship was laden with spices and animals, each pungent and new. The captain sold a monkey to a lady on the riverbank, who took it home to the big house, letting it ride on her shoulder in the carriage and calling it by the name of her uncle, who looked the same.

The ship still stands by the river, its wide canvas mainsail fastened to the mast like a white starched blouse clasped with a golden safety pin. Ropes and rigging are tied to the wood with hooks and special knots which all have names:

hitch, eye, slip and hoop. It looks like a ship in a bottle, made from matchsticks and the bones from a rabbit, and small pieces of calico cut from a best petticoat.

Today the tide is out, revealing the riverbed, deep with sludge. The stench of it agitates the dogs on the bank, making them bark harder. It is stagnant, still. Green scum left behind by the receding water kisses the boats, tied up to the bank wall and abandoned. Their white and blue hulls are silt-sunk until the incoming tide floats them again, down the river and into the sea.

Where the river meets the bank, there's a round maw in the wall. Here, grime pours from the city. Moving slowly through the sewer where rats squeal in the darkness, a swollen lump of congealed fat makes its way to the river – a galleon sailing through an icy sea. Rotten and growing, gathering old oil, grease from meat and potatoes, offal from pies, gristly shavings from kebabs. The fat is moving – it smells the sea and creeps closer to the mouth cut in the riverbank. It looks out at the world – at the water and the weather, at the train as it crosses the bridge.

The Bridge

The train moves across the river, up high on the suspended track, paused in time – not in the water, not in the air, not in the city. The muddy waters ebb below. As the train makes the crossing, the wind blows up the river and buffets the carriage, playing with its prey. It flutters the coloured ribbons tied to the bridge railing alongside other trinkets – gewgaws, tassels and rosettes – moving silently in the winter breeze. The wind carries the sound of ancient music, written when tunes had fewer notes – plucked on a lyre and a lute, played on a crumhorn in a wood-panelled hall, on feasts and high days when the table was piled with sweetmeats and marchpane moulded into the shape of a swan. Figs, eels in aspic, tongue, baked apples and a great roasted boar – eyes melted shut.

On the train, a man pulls a coin from his pocket and rubs it frantically on a deck of silvered scratchcards – itching the scab on his life until his whole lap is covered with useless scales. A wrinkled shark swims down his arm – once black, now copper green.

A whale takes a wrong turning at the river-mouth and swims towards the city. Confused by the noise, it stops and lies on the silty bottom. It is remembering. Out in the wide ocean it swam with brothers and sisters, hundreds of them, gathered in a place not marked on any map – a place they felt with the compasses inside them, the needles quivering, jumping to the beat of their giant hearts. They came in vast schools – from warm island waters filled with rainbow coral and anemones, from the frozen waters of the north, where the sea is crowned with ice. Together they swam with the octopus and squid, in a circle a mile wide, beating their tails and frothing the water blue to white, whisking a cocktail filled with prawns and silver fish.

Old hulks, anchored, creak and bang metallically out in the middle of the river. The water is too warm for the whale, and too shallow. Green fingers of riverbed weed sway towards the surface, tickling its belly. The whale is exhausted, terrified of beaching in the shallows. It likes the cold water of the open sea, where there are deep waves it can hide in. People gather on the bridge. Waving, and taking pictures with small black boxes which flash like ship lights in the dark ocean. The whale starts to cry, tears mixing with the brine.

The City

A woman stares out the window without seeing the view. She wears a black and white uniform, her name stitched across the shirt pocket. Her nail varnish is chipped and her hair is tumbling out of the band she has gathered it in. She's earning to feed her baby girl, who she decorates with a big pink bow, tied round her head like a candied tourniquet – a sweet bandage to hold her brain in place.

She'll step out of the winter gloom into the dry heat of the salon, swapping fleece-lined slipper booties for hard wooden clogs. She'll tear paper from the roll and pull it over the daybed – theatrical hygiene, betrayed by the brown stain in the ceiling panels her clients see when they lie down. That's all they can see, that stain. She'll heat the pale pink wax in a pot, stirring it like porridge. Her clients wince and buck as she rips out their hair, and she watches the tears swell in their eyes, reflecting her own sallow face. She tosses the wax strips in the bin – hairy animals caught in a sticky trap.

Into the tunnel. Winter daylight is rapidly extinguished, replaced by blackened brick. The soil around the walls is packed tight, filled with larvae and rasping pink earthworms. Above, buildings sprout from vacant lots. Looming glass temples and gleaming blocks shrink old churches and raze dilapidated pubs, filling the spaces with meetings and progress.

The train re-emerges – an insect from a cocoon – into the shadow of the tallest tower. A glazed fortress, a counter-point to trees and animals, a shining beacon of commerce. A rook complains about the cold, and the wind throws its voice against the building. Two men with sponges dangle in a metal basket slung on a rope, wiping dirt from the reflective walls. Their cage swings violently – a crow's nest moving in a storm.

A beggar kneels on the pavement outside, rocking back and forth, her rhythm marking the desperate tick of her clock, which will stop short. Through frosted lenses, she sees only light and shadow. Most people walk past, turning their blind eyes away from hers. Some stop, briefly, paying for their guilt by pressing golden coins into her feeling hands or dropping them into her cup. She blesses them

– her mouth makes the shape of a prayer and her hands paint a cross on the air. She holds a cardboard message in place with her bare toes, blackened by the dirty ground and the cruelty of the city, and pleads for help of any kind – food, water, silver, prayers – pointing to her mouth with a crooked finger. A woman stops and pulls a red apple from her bag like a witch in a fairytale.

The train reaches the big station and the people pour across the concourse – a flood of souls swimming through streets and passageways, dissipating into the fog. Human liquid borne ceaselessly forward.

In the evening they regroup, iron filings drawn to a magnet which sucks them home – where they lie awake in the early hours of the morning, where they collect their belongings and their memories, where the day turns into night.

The End

Some people buy tickets for a seat a mile up, drinking apple schnapps as they fly to the iciest mountains, or tread wooden decks in bare feet as they sail over the waves to hot jungles. Others take the train, staring through the window – writing stories on the landscape, watching, wondering.

Past the cottages at the end of the village, past the big house on the hill, through the wood and past the chalk pit, past the cemetery, past the power station and the flats, into the city. Look, here are all the little places, announced over and over, until they are just sounds – no longer words but the chimes of a bell, ringing from a steeple.

THE END

Acknowledgements

This book began as a way of making my long weekday commute less painful, when someone kind suggested I should try writing about it. Back then, my tired old laptop died within seconds when it wasn't plugged in, so I had no choice but to write by hand.

I filled four notebooks and eleven months with all the words inside me, writing stories about *All The Little Places* I saw from the train window – writing my way out of my morning funk, following the track through my own journey.

Creating a book is not a solo endeavour. I am profoundly grateful to Toby at Blue Mark Books for having faith in my writing, and for all his hard work and expertise. Knowing he would sew a pocket in the world in which to fold my words gave purpose and meaning to them.

I would like to thank Mark at Mecob, who made the excellent drawings in this book and designed the cover.

I think he might secretly have been sitting in the same carriage, seeing just what I saw.

Some more thank yous: to my early readers – Carol, Fiona, Gina, Jayne, and Mum – for taking the time and trouble to labour through early drafts that weren't quite shiny enough, and for all your support and encouragement. In particular to David who, as always, had some brilliantly radical ideas. To all those friends who graciously suffered impromptu, lubricated readings – apologies.

And to my critical friend – thank you for making this book, like everything else, so much better.